Tom Sawyer

MARK TWAIN

SADDLEBACK
EDUCATIONAL PUBLISHING

Saddleback's *Illustrated Classics*™

Three Watson
Irvine, CA 92618-2767
Website: www.sdlback.com

ISBN-13: 978-1-56254-946-6
ISBN-10: 1-56254-946-4
eBook: 978-1-60291-172-7

Printed in China

12 11 10 09 08 9 8 7 6 5 4 3

Welcome to
Saddleback's *Illustrated Classics*™

We are proud to welcome you to Saddleback's *Illustrated Classics*™. Saddleback's *Illustrated Classics*™ was designed specifically for the classroom to introduce readers to many of the great classics in literature. Each text, written and adapted by teachers and researchers, has been edited using the Dale-Chall vocabulary system. In addition, much time and effort has been spent to ensure that these high-interest stories retain all of the excitement, intrigue, and adventure of the original books.

With these graphically *Illustrated Classics*™, you learn what happens in the story in a number of different ways. One way is by reading the words a character says. Another way is by looking at the drawings of the character. The artist can tell you what kind of person a character is and what he or she is thinking or feeling.

This series will help you to develop confidence and a sense of accomplishment as you finish each novel. The stories in Saddleback's *Illustrated Classics*™ are fun to read. And remember, fun motivates!

Overview

Everyone deserves to read the best literature our language has to offer. Saddleback's *Illustrated Classics*™ was designed to acquaint readers with the most famous stories from the world's greatest authors, while teaching essential skills. You will learn how to:

- Establish a purpose for reading
- Use prior knowledge
- Evaluate your reading
- Listen to the language as it is written
- Extend literary and language appreciation through discussion and writing activities

Reading is one of the most important skills you will ever learn. It provides the key to all kinds of information. By reading the *Illustrated Classics*™, you will develop confidence and the self-satisfaction that comes from accomplishment— a solid foundation for any reader.

Step-By-Step

The following is a simple guide to using and enjoying each of your *Illustrated Classics™*. To maximize your use of the learning activities provided, we suggest that you follow these steps:

1. ***Listen!*** We suggest that you listen to the read-along. (At this time, please ignore the beeps.) You will enjoy this wonderfully dramatized presentation.

2. ***Pre-reading Activities.*** After listening to the audio presentation, the pre-reading activities in the Activity Book prepare you for reading the story by setting the scene, introducing more difficult vocabulary words, and providing some short exercises.

3. ***Reading Activities.*** Now turn to the "While you are reading" portion of the Activity Book, which directs you to make a list of story-related facts. Read-along while listening to the audio presentation. (This time pay attention to the beeps, as they indicate when each page should be turned.)

4. ***Post-reading Activities.*** You have successfully read the story and listened to the audio presentation. Now answer the multiple-choice questions and other activities in the Activity Book.

Remember,

"Today's readers are tomorrow's leaders."

ABOUT THE AUTHOR

If Huckleberry Finn is the embodiment of American boyhood, Tom Sawyer is the embodiment of any imagination or mischief that Huckleberry lacked.

Twain, himself, grew up in Missouri and early developed a lively spirit of adventure. He transmitted this spirit to his characters in a highly readable and sensitive style.

Twain has a gift for combining the humorous with the serious. His characters are real and believable; his settings are natural. He entertains while he instructs, a trait for which the ancients would praise him.

Other books by Twain include *Pudd'nhead Wilson, Life on the Mississippi, The Prince and the Pauper, A Connecticut Yankee in King Arthur's Court,* and *The Celebrated Jumping Frog of Calavares County* (his first).

Saddleback's *Illustrated Classics*™

Tom Sawyer

MARK TWAIN

THE MAIN CHARACTERS

Becky Thatcher

Huck Finn

Tom Sawyer

Aunt Polly

Injun Joe

When Samuel Clemens (better known as Mark Twain) had become a famous writer, he remembered growing up in a small town on the Mississippi River. From the things that happened to him as a boy, he made up Tom Sawyer and other characters that will be remembered for a long time. . .Huck Finn, Aunt Polly, Becky Thatcher, Injun Joe, and others. Here are the adventures of Tom Sawyer. . .adventures that meant fun and joy, danger and fear, and even death to some.

Clemens began his story with Tom's Aunt Polly.

Tom! Tom! If I get hold of you, I'll. . .I never did see the best of that boy!

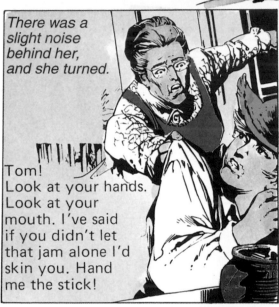

There was a slight noise behind her, and she turned.

Tom! Look at your hands. Look at your mouth. I've said if you didn't let that jam alone I'd skin you. Hand me the stick!

Look behind you, Aunt!

Aunt Polly turned around quickly, and, in an instant, the boy fled.

Hang the boy! He played enough tricks like that on me to be caught and punished this time!

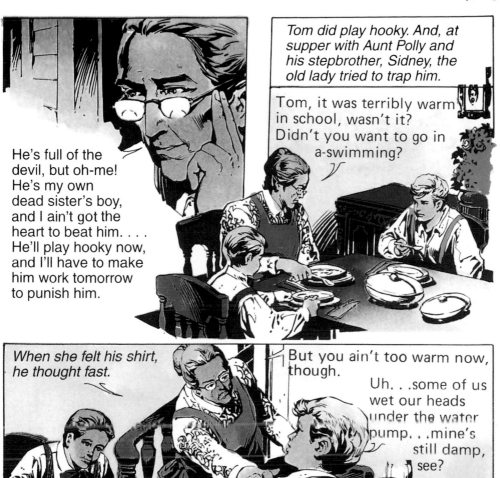

Tom did play hooky. And, at supper with Aunt Polly and his stepbrother, Sidney, the old lady tried to trap him.

Tom, it was terribly warm in school, wasn't it? Didn't you want to go in a-swimming?

He's full of the devil, but oh-me! He's my own dead sister's boy, and I ain't got the heart to beat him. . . . He'll play hooky now, and I'll have to make him work tomorrow to punish him.

When she felt his shirt, he thought fast.

But you ain't too warm now, though.

Uh. . .some of us wet our heads under the water pump. . .mine's still damp, see?

No'm. It's still sewed! I'll show you!

Tom, you didn't have to unbutton your shirt collar, where I sewed it, did you?

Well, now, I thought you sewed his collar in white thread, but now it's black.

Why, I did sew it with white! Tom, you went swimming, then sewed your collar up yourself!

Siddy, I'll get you for that!

The next day came Aunt Polly's punishment . . .painting the back fence.

Jeepers, it'll take me all day!

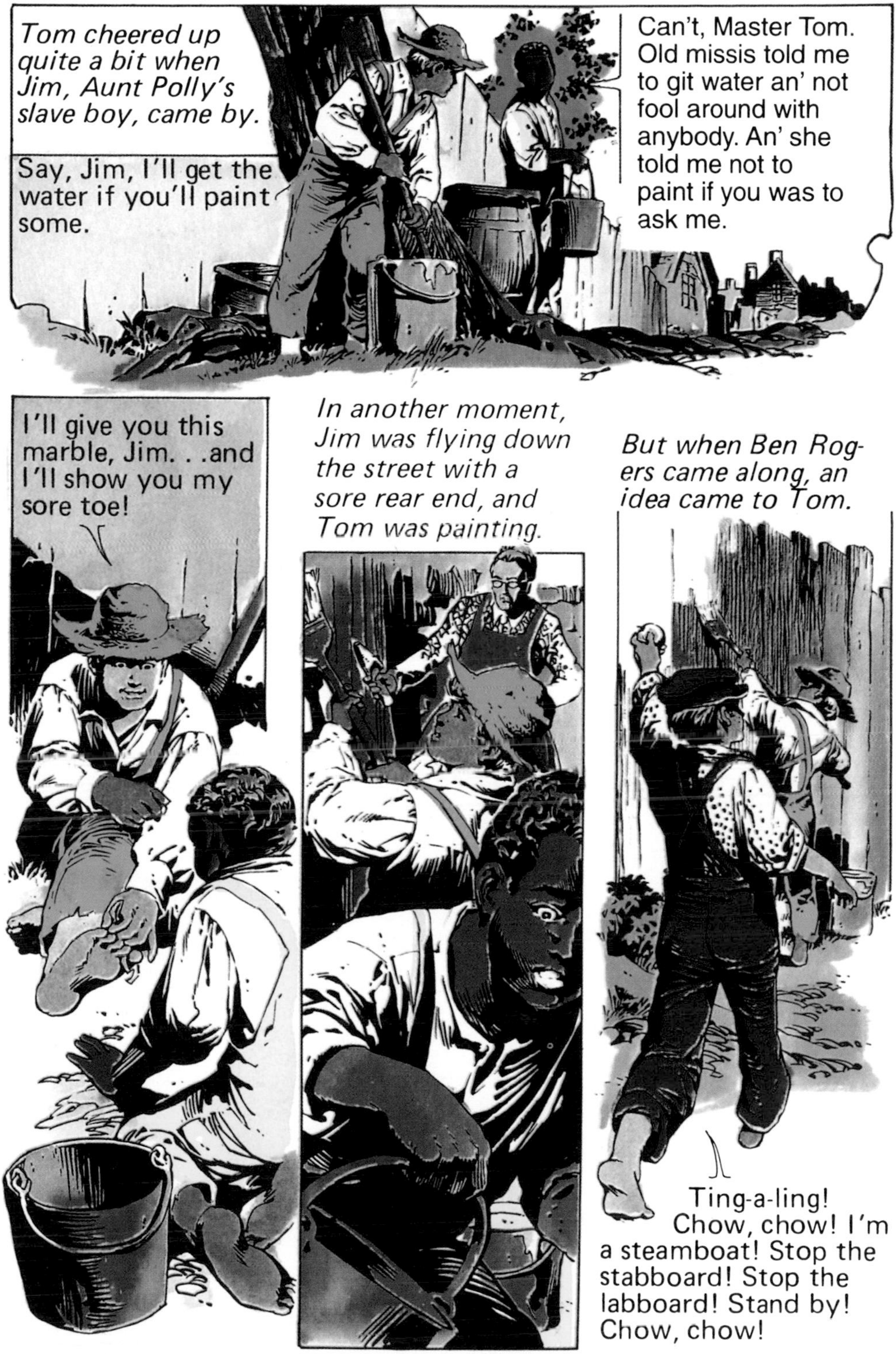
Tom cheered up quite a bit when Jim, Aunt Polly's slave boy, came by.
Say, Jim, I'll get the water if you'll paint some.
Can't, Master Tom. Old missis told me to git water an' not fool around with anybody. An' she told me not to paint if you was to ask me.
I'll give you this marble, Jim. . .and I'll show you my sore toe!
In another moment, Jim was flying down the street with a sore rear end, and Tom was painting.
But when Ben Rogers came along, an idea came to Tom.
Ting-a-ling! Chow, chow! I'm a steamboat! Stop the stabboard! Stop the labboard! Stand by! Chow, chow!

Got to work, hey? I'm going swimming. . . but, of course, you'd rather work, wouldn't you?

Oh, I don't call this work! It's fine with me!

You mean you like it?

Why not? Does a boy get a chance to paint a fence every day?

Before long. . . .

Er. . .say, Tom, let me paint a little.

No, no. . .it's got to be done very careful. I reckon there ain't but one boy in a thousand that can do it right.

Let me try, won't you? Say. . . I'll give you my apple!

Well. . .I shouldn't but. . .all right.

Other boys came to laugh, but stayed to paint.

Let me try it, Tom!

No, me, Tom!

By afternoon, Tom had a pile of gifts, and the fence had three coats of paint. He had discovered a great law. Work is made up of whatever a person has to do; play is made up of whatever a person wants to do.

Tom collected a further reward. . . .

Well, I never! It just shows. . you can work when you want to! Let me give you a nice apple, then go 'long and play.

But before he went out to play, Tom gave a little punishment of his own.

Ow! Aunt Polly!

That's for tellin' about the black thread!

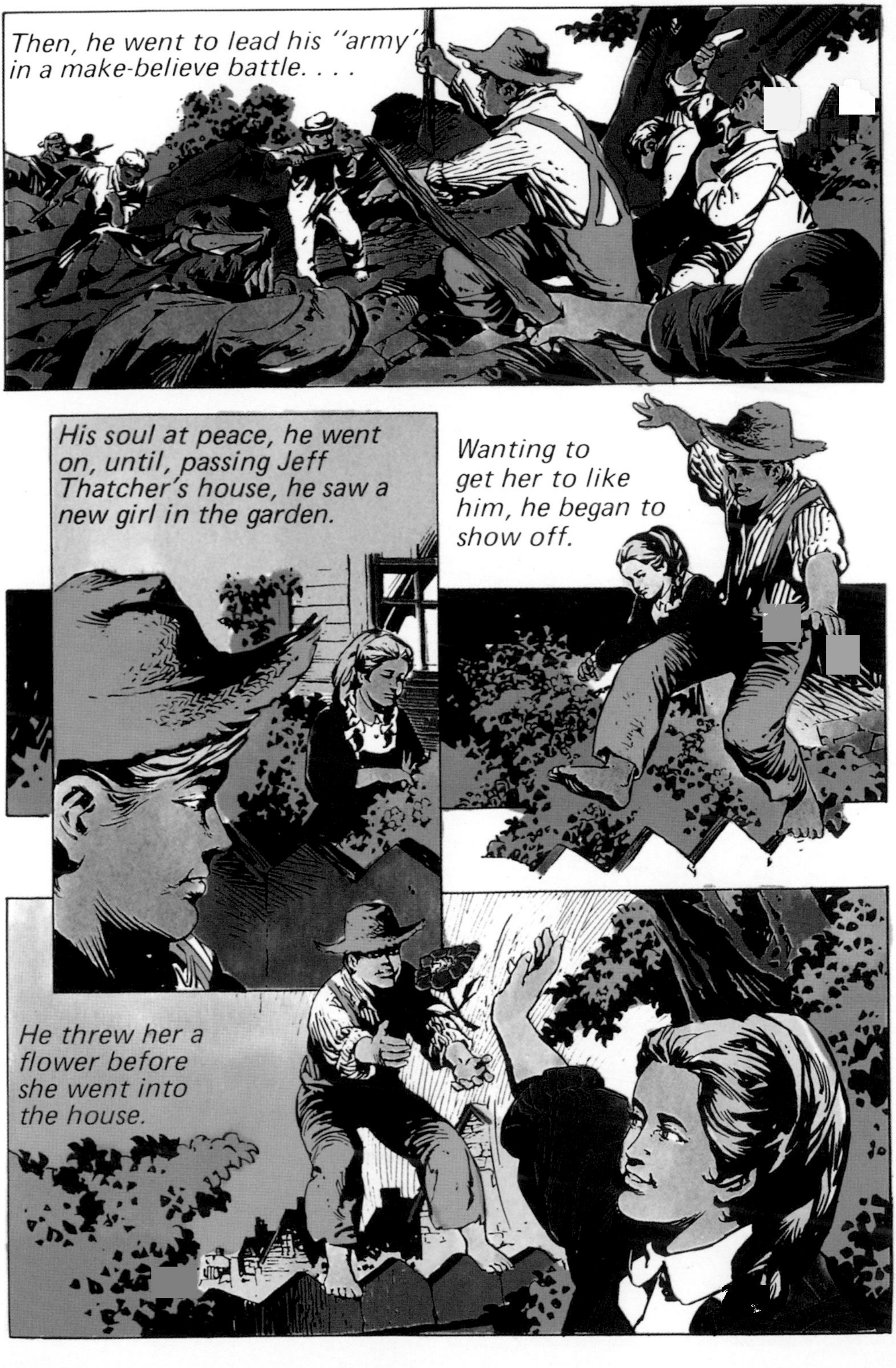
Then, he went to lead his "army" in a make-believe battle. . . .
His soul at peace, he went on, until, passing Jeff Thatcher's house, he saw a new girl in the garden.
Wanting to get her to like him, he began to show off.
He threw her a flower before she went into the house.

And when he got home, his head full of dreams. . . .

Tom, here's your cousin Mary, back from her trip to the country. . . Why, what's got into you, Tom?

Sigh!

The next day was Sunday, which meant church and Sunday school.

Why do they make clothes like this anyway?

Huckleberry Finn, the son of the town drunkard, was an outcast. He was loved by all the children, who wished they dared be like him.

Then, Monday, on his way to school. . . .

Hello, Huckleberry!

What's that you've got?

Hello yourself, and see how you like it!

Dead cat. Good to cure warts with.

Say, Hucky, when are you going to try the cat?

Tonight. I reckon the devil will come after old Hoss Williams.

You take it to the graveyard about midnight when somebody that was wicked was buried. Devils will come to take the body away. You throw the cat after him and say, "Devil follow dead man, cat follow devil, warts follow cat, I'm done with you." That'll get rid of any wart.

Lemme go with you!

Sure. . .if you ain't afeared. I'll meow under your window.

Reaching the little frame schoolhouse, Tom walked in briskly.

Thomas Sawyer! Come up here. Why are you late again, as usual?

Tom was ready to lie, when he saw his Loved One. . .and next to her the only empty place on the girls' side.

It's her!

Sitting next to her, Tom soon learned that her name was Becky Thatcher. She soon learned something, too.

I LOVE YOU

I stopped to talk to Huckleberry Finn!

This is the most surprising confession I ever heard! After I hit you, go and sit with the girls!

At noon, while the other children went home, they stayed behind, and. . .

Say, Becky, let's get engaged to be married!

It sounds nice . . .but I never heard of it before.

Oh, it's ever so gay! Why me and Amy Lawrence. . . .

Oh, Tom! Then I ain't the first you've ever been engaged to!

But I don't care for her anymore!

You do! Go away! And never talk to me again!

Tom was very sad, nevertheless, he didn't forget his meeting with Huck Finn that night.

Meow! Meow!

That's Huck! Time to go!

Meow!

Meow!

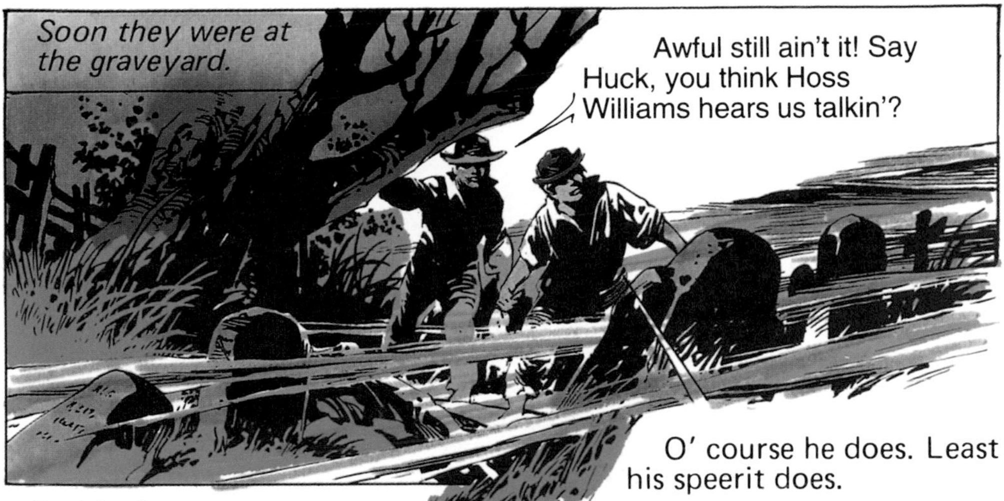
Soon they were at the graveyard.
Awful still ain't it! Say Huck, you think Hoss Williams hears us talkin'?
O' course he does. Least his speerit does.

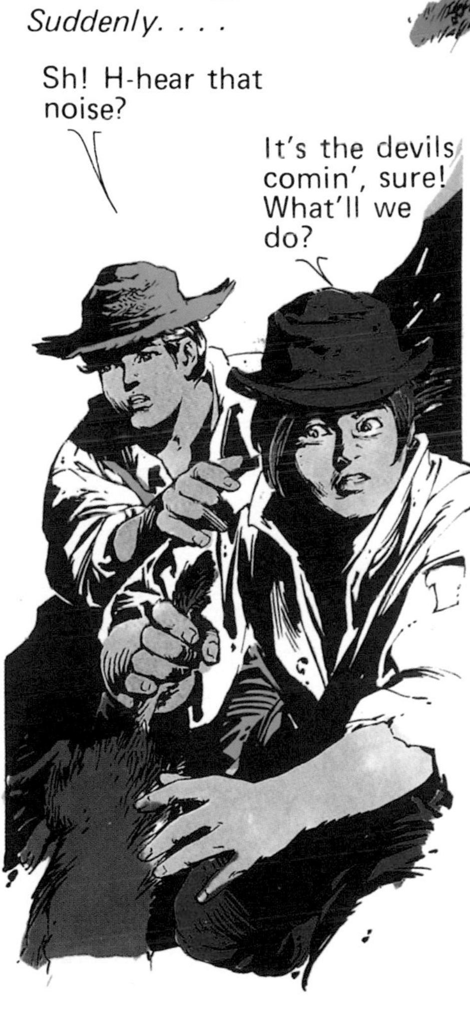
Suddenly. . . .
Sh! H-hear that noise?
It's the devils comin', sure! What'll we do?

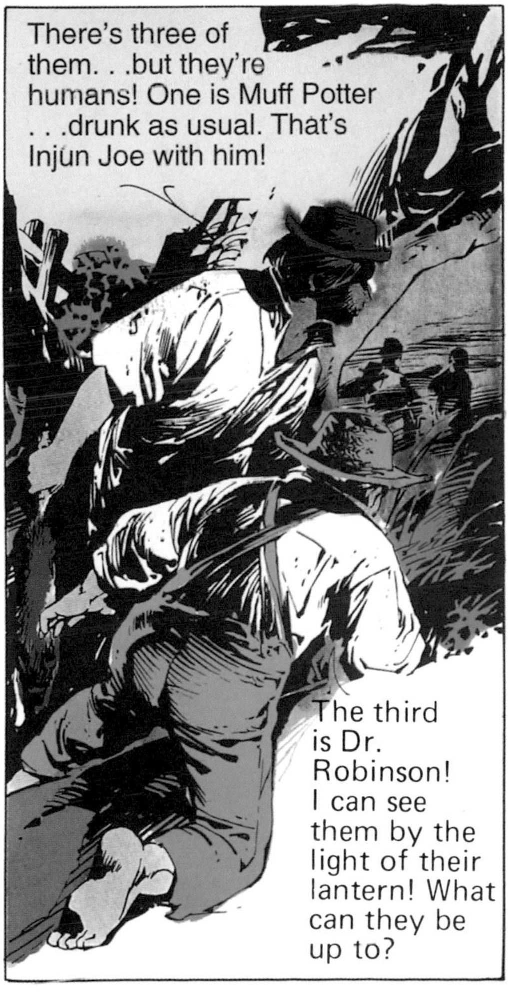
There's three of them. . .but they're humans! One is Muff Potter . . .drunk as usual. That's Injun Joe with him!
The third is Dr. Robinson! I can see them by the light of their lantern! What can they be up to?

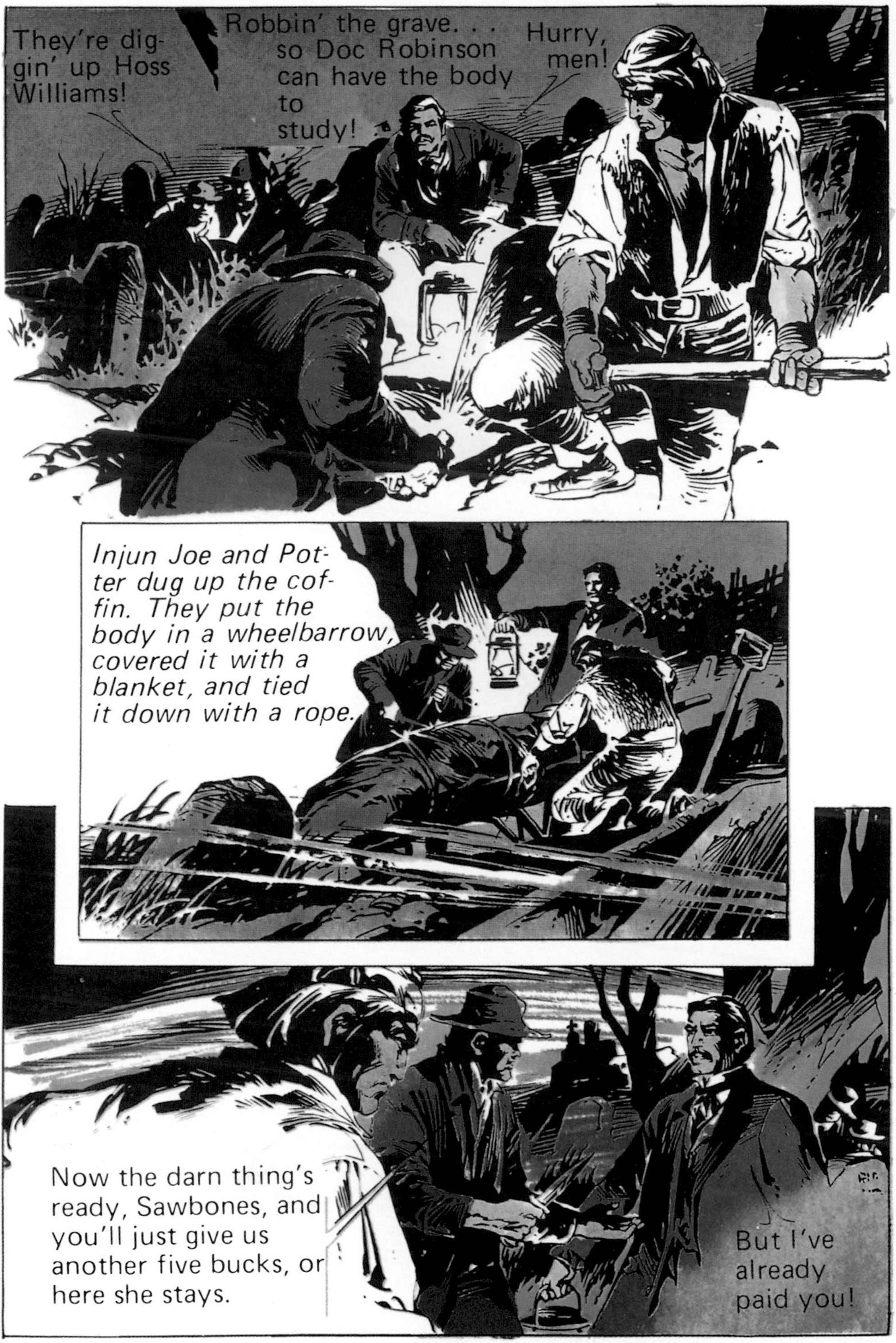
They're dig-
gin' up Hoss
Williams!
Robbin' the grave. . .
so Doc Robinson
can have the body
to
study!
Hurry,
men!
Injun Joe and Pot-
ter dug up the cof-
fin. They put the
body in a wheelbarrow,
covered it with a
blanket, and tied
it down with a rope.
Now the darn thing's
ready, Sawbones, and
you'll just give us
another five bucks, or
here she stays.
But I've
already
paid you!

I ain't forgot that five years ago you drove me away from your father's kitchen, then your father had me jailed for a bum. Now I've got you, and you got to settle, you know!

The doctor struck out suddenly at Injun Joe.

Here, now, don't hit my partner!

As the doctor fought with Potter, Injun Joe picked up the knife.

Then the doctor knocked Potter down with the headstone of the grave.

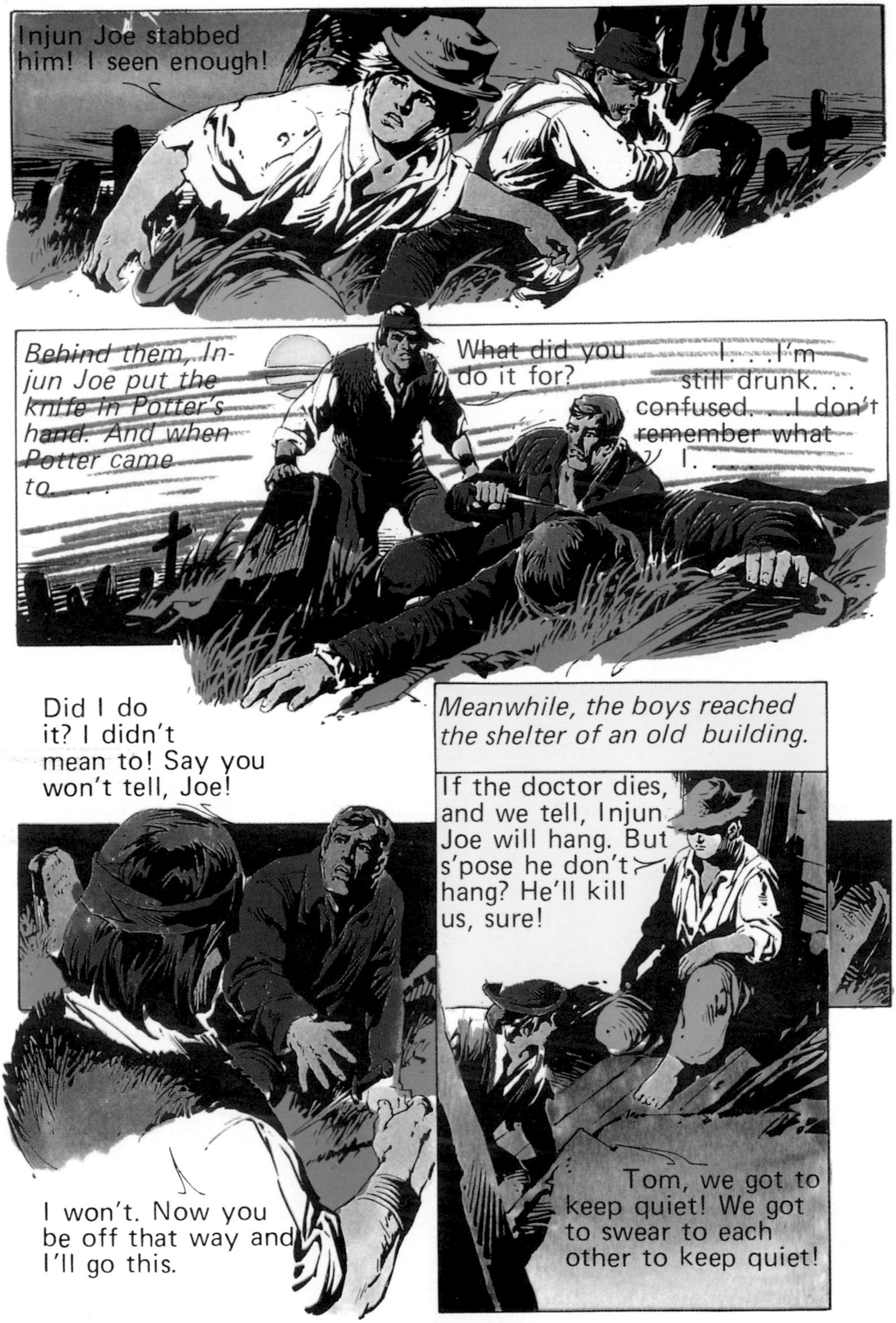
Injun Joe stabbed him! I seen enough!
Behind them, Injun Joe put the knife in Potter's hand. And when Potter came to. . . .
What did you do it for?
I. . .I'm still drunk. . . confused. . .I don't remember what I. . . .
Did I do it? I didn't mean to! Say you won't tell, Joe!
I won't. Now you be off that way and I'll go this.
Meanwhile, the boys reached the shelter of an old building.
If the doctor dies, and we tell, Injun Joe will hang. But s'pose he don't hang? He'll kill us, sure!
Tom, we got to keep quiet! We got to swear to each other to keep quiet!

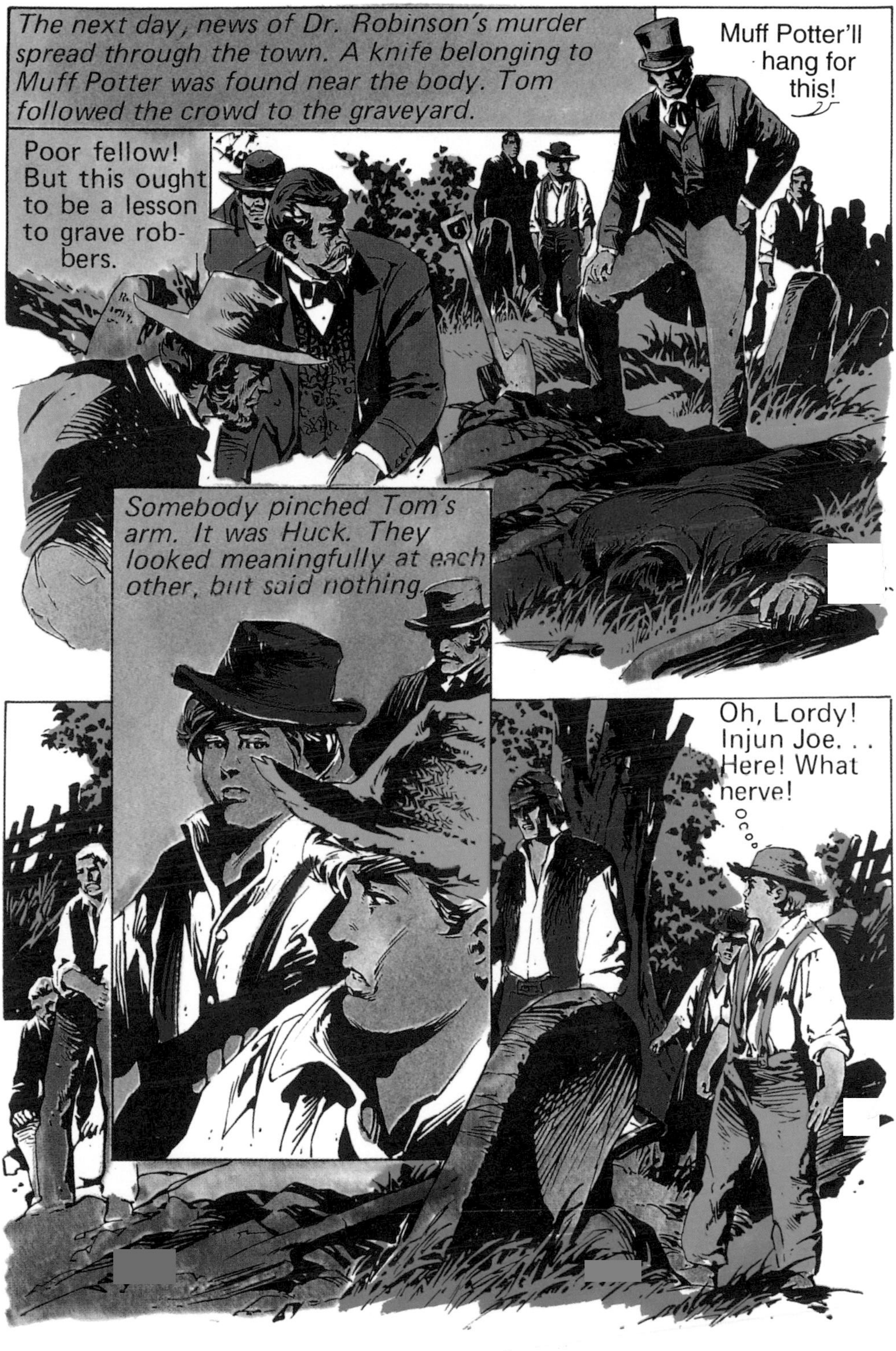
The next day, news of Dr. Robinson's murder spread through the town. A knife belonging to Muff Potter was found near the body. Tom followed the crowd to the graveyard.
Muff Potter'll hang for this!
Poor fellow! But this ought to be a lesson to grave robbers.
Somebody pinched Tom's arm. It was Huck. They looked meaningfully at each other, but said nothing.
Oh, Lordy! Injun Joe. . . Here! What nerve!

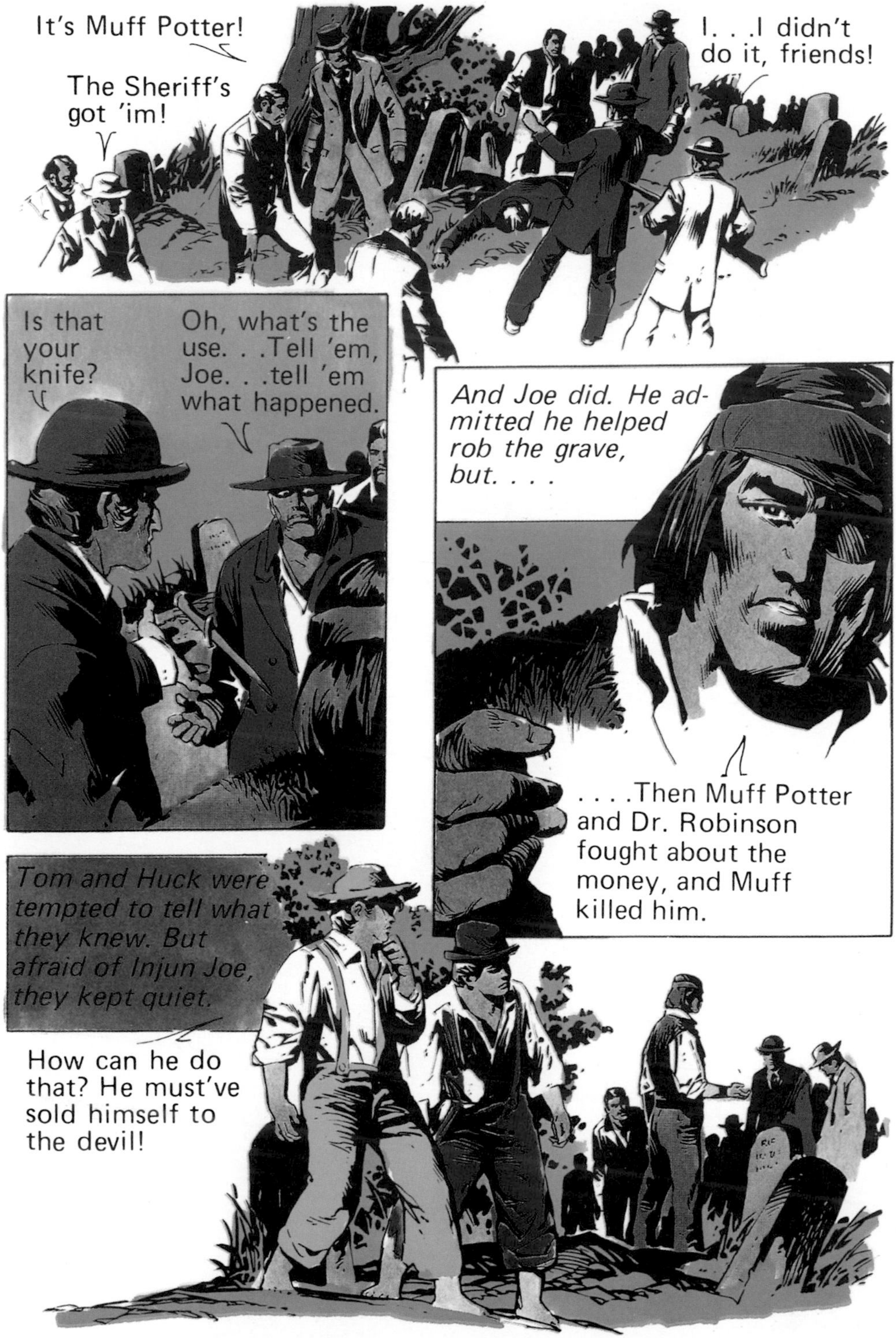
It's Muff Potter!
The Sheriff's got 'im!
I. . .I didn't do it, friends!
Is that your knife?
Oh, what's the use. . .Tell 'em, Joe. . .tell 'em what happened.
And Joe did. He admitted he helped rob the grave, but. . . .
. . . .Then Muff Potter and Dr. Robinson fought about the money, and Muff killed him.
Tom and Huck were tempted to tell what they knew. But afraid of Injun Joe, they kept quiet.
How can he do that? He must've sold himself to the devil!

During the days that followed, Tom brought small things to Potter when he could get hold of them.

Thank you kindly, son.

Before long, another, more important matter was on his mind. Becky Thatcher was ill. He took to hanging around her father's house at night.

Oh, I can't stand this! I hope she gets better. . .fast.

Seeing how sad and worried he was, Aunt Polly fed him Painkiller, her favorite medicine.

Ugh! It tastes terrible! It'll kill me!

Nonsense! It will do you good!

Tom, of course, fed it to the cat!

Look at him go!

Then one day at school. . . .

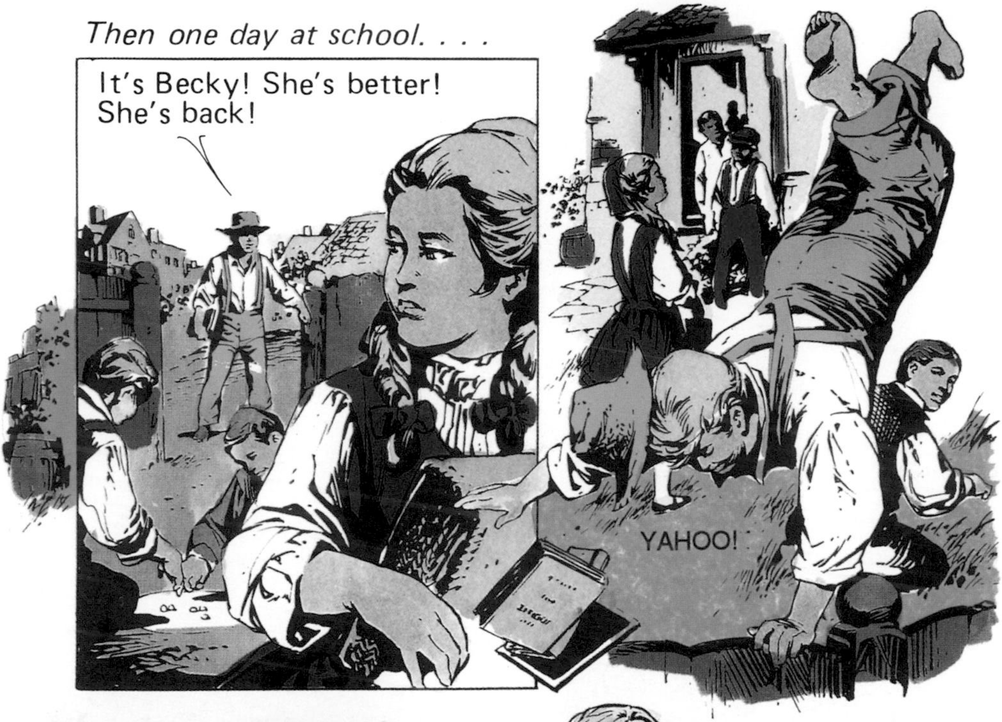
It's Becky! She's better! She's back!
YAHOO!

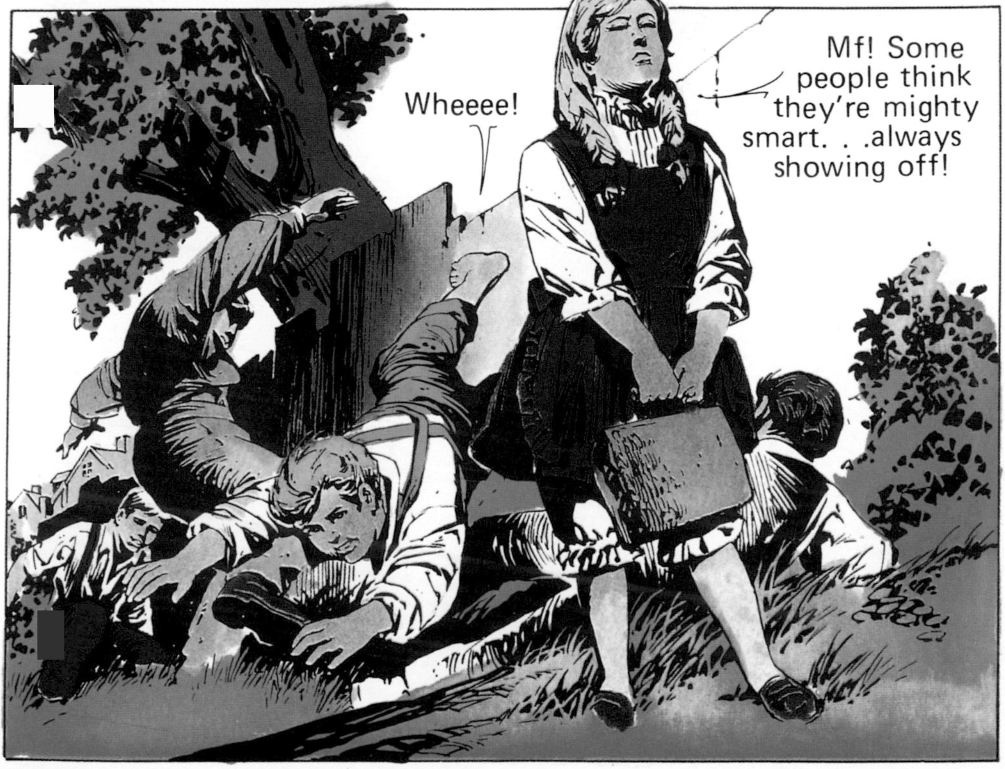
Wheeee!
Mf! Some people think they're mighty smart. . .always showing off!

Tom sneaked off. . . heartbroken.

I'll run off, that's what! Then they'll all be sorry!

He soon met his good friend, Joe Harper, and found that they were two boys with the same idea.

Nobody cares for me here, Joe . . .so I'm running away.

So am I. Ma whipped me for drinking some cream, and I never touched it.

Let's go together. We can go to Jackson's Island . . .nobody lives there We'll be hermits.

No, pirates. We'll ask Huck Finn to come with us.

Huck agreed. Carrying supplies they had stolen, they met on the riverbank, where there was a raft they could capture. Tom answered their whistle, and. . . .

This is the Black Avenger of the Spanish Main. Name your names.

Joe Harper, the Terror of the Sea!

Huck Finn the Red-Handed!

'Tis well. Give the password.

They quickly jumped on the raft and made their way three miles down the river to the island where no one lived.

Leaving the raft on a sandbar, they hid their supplies, then went to sleep in the open, as outlaws should.

In the morning, they break-fasted on fish caught in the river.

They went looking around and found that the raft had floated away. Later, they heard a boom from the distance.

M-m-m. . .Best fish I ever tasted.

What's that?

I wonder. . . Let's go see!

I know now! Somebody's drownded!

That's it! They shoot a cannon over the water, and that makes him come to the top.

I'd give anything to know who it is.

I know. . . it's us! They found the raft and think we drownded!

At first they felt like heroes. But, as night came on, they had second thoughts.

Ma must be feelin' bad.

And my Aunt Polly, too.

That night, when the others were asleep, Tom went off.

He sneaked a free ride across the river. . . .

. . . .and made his way to Aunt Polly's house. There she sat, with Joe Harper's mother, Sid, and Mary.

It was just so with my Joe.

Tom wasn't so bad. . .only silly and full of mischief . . .and the best-hearted boy that ever was.

Quietly, he slipped inside. . . .

. . . .and hid under the bed.

Poor boys! If the bodies are missing till Sunday, the funerals will be held that morning.

Tom had to wait until Aunt Polly was asleep. Then, before he left, he kissed the kindly old lady.

Dear Aunt Polly! She really cares for me!

After Tom returned to the island, the boys fished and swam and played games.

But later, they were very homesick.

I want to go home. It's so lonesome here.

Let's go too, Tom!

Go on, then! I'm staying!

As Joe and Huck began to leave. . .

Wait! Wait! I want to tell you something!

Tom told his secret plan, and the others set up a war whoop telling Tom how great it was.

That's a great plan, Tom! Why didn't you tell us before?

And so they all stayed. . .and that night were terrified by a storm.

The next day, the storm over, they cheered themselves by being Indians instead of pirates.

On Sunday, the little church in town was packed for the funeral service. Moved by the sermon, the whole church wept. . .even the preacher himself.

Suddenly the church door creaked, and the three dead boys came marching up the aisle. They had been hiding in the empty balcony, listening to their own funeral.

Aunt Polly, Mary, and the Harpers threw themselves upon their boys.

As a hymn filled the church, Tom confessed in his heart that this was the proudest moment of his life.

Praise God. . .and put your hearts into it!

At school, Tom and Joe were heroes. Tom pretended not to see Becky. He'd show he could live without her!

But after he had seen her pay attention to another boy. . . .

Tell us more about the island, Tom!

I acted mighty mean Becky, and I'm sorry. Please make up, won't you?

I'll thank you to keep yourself to yourself, Mr. Thomas Sawyer! I'll never speak to you again!

Soon after, Tom found her, looking in the schoolmaster's anatomy book. As she quickly put it away, a page tore.

Oh, I tore it, and I'll be whipped! It's your fault. . . sneaking up on me!

I didn't! But you'll get a beating, all right!

Sure enough, Becky could not hide her guilt from the searching look of the schoolmaster.

Who tore this book? . . .Rebecca Thatcher, look me in the face!

But before she could confess. . . .

She didn't do it! I done it!

Tom's punishment was swift. . . but so was his reward.

Tom, how could you be so kind!

Vacation time came, and Becky was away with her family. Quiet days. . .until the murder trial came up in court.

Muff Potter will hang for certain.

He deserves it!

As the trial went on, Tom's conscience bothered him.

I guess Muff is a goner. But what can we do?

Not a thing. If we talk, Injun Joe will kill us, sure as shootin'. We better keep quiet, like we swore.

Tom hung around the courtroom but didn't go in. He heard troubling news.

Think the jury will find Potter guilty?

They'll have to . . .you heard Injun Joe's evidence.

Tom was out late that night. He had something very important to do. He came to bed through the window, very excited.

Huck won't like it. . .but I had to do it!

The next day, Potter's lawyer surprised everyone in court.

I ask Thomas Sawyer be called to the stand as a witness.

Every eye was on Tom as he took his place on the stand.

Thomas Sawyer, where were you on the 17th of June, about the hour of midnight!

In the graveyard.

Were you anywhere near Hoss Williams' grave?

Yes, sir. I was hid behind the elm trees on the edge of the grave.

Tom told the whole story of what he had seen, and as he reached the end... Look out!

...then Injun Joe jumped with the knife, and...

Injun Joe's gettin' away!

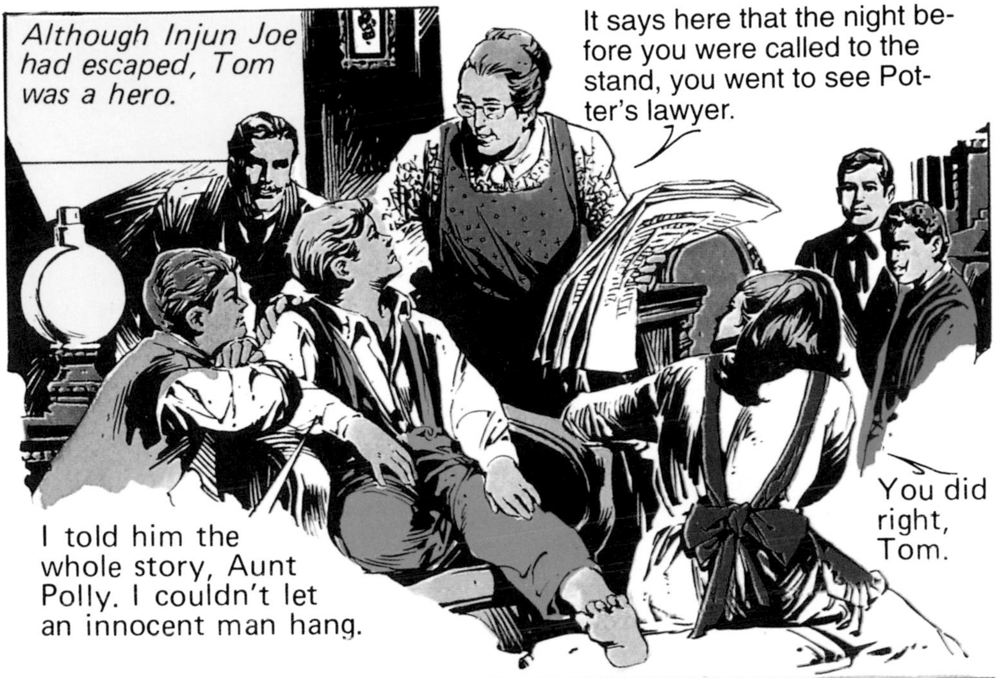
Although Injun Joe had escaped, Tom was a hero.
It says here that the night before you were called to the stand, you went to see Potter's lawyer.
I told him the whole story, Aunt Polly. I couldn't let an innocent man hang.
You did right, Tom.

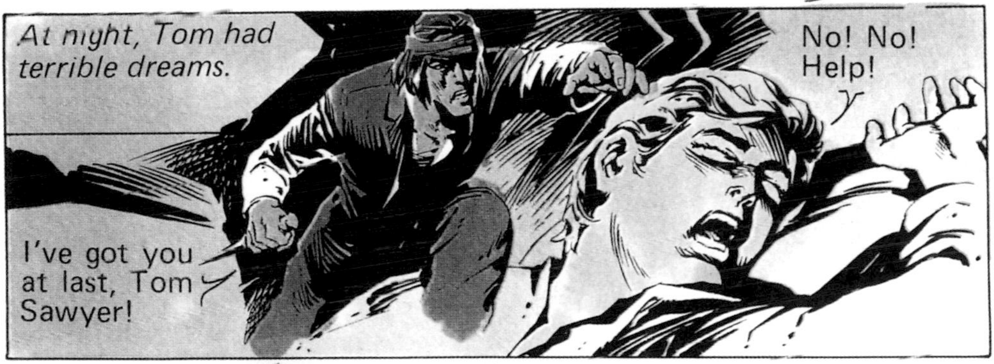
At night, Tom had terrible dreams.
No! No! Help!
I've got you at last, Tom Sawyer!

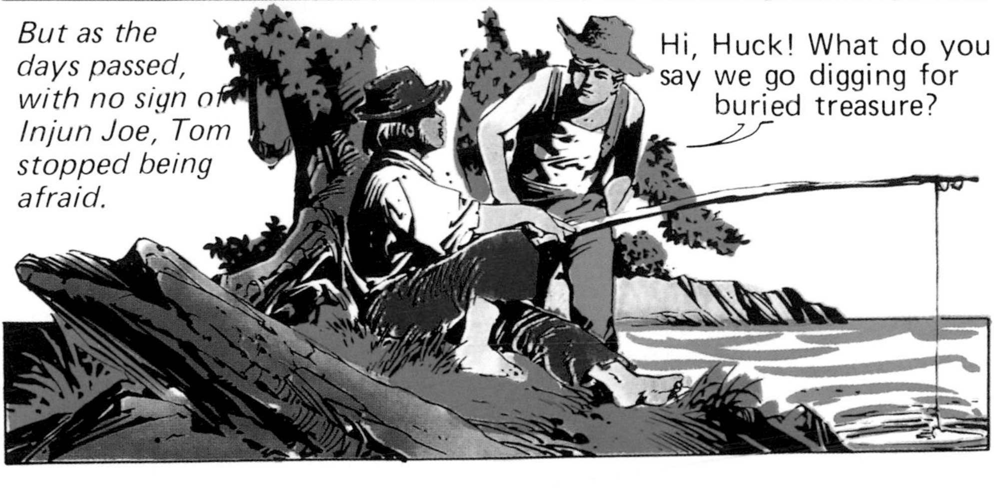
But as the days passed, with no sign of Injun Joe, Tom stopped being afraid.
Hi, Huck! What do you say we go digging for buried treasure?

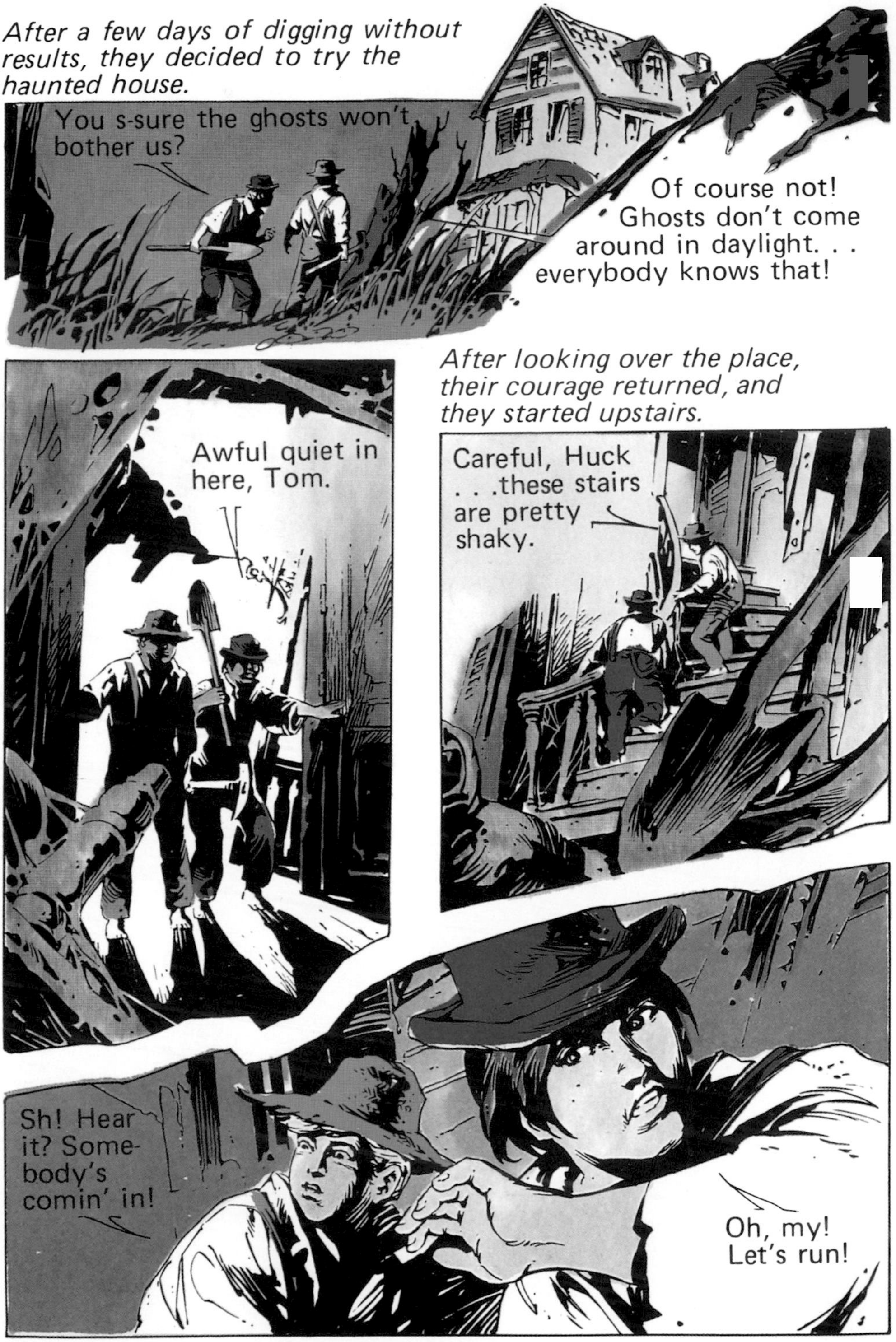
After a few days of digging without results, they decided to try the haunted house.
You s-sure the ghosts won't bother us?
Of course not! Ghosts don't come around in daylight. . . everybody knows that!
Awful quiet in here, Tom.
After looking over the place, their courage returned, and they started upstairs.
Careful, Huck . . .these stairs are pretty shaky.
Sh! Hear it? Somebody's comin' in!
Oh, my! Let's run!

Keep still! We can watch them through the holes in the floor.

There's two of them! One's the old deaf-and-dumb Spaniard that's been in town once or twice lately. . .never saw the other man before.

While the boys watched from above, the two men spoke of dangerous jobs they meant to do.

The deaf-and-dumb Spaniard spoke. . . and the boys knew his voice.

It's Injun Joe!

What'll we do with the money? We've got six hundred and fifty in silver.

Bury it. . . right here.

42

Wait! I hit some- thing. . .a rotten plank. No, it's a box! I broke a hole in it! Let's see what's in it!

Man, it's money . . .gold!

We'll do this quickly. There's a pick an' shovel in the corner. . .I saw them a minute ago.

The box was soon dug up.

Partner, there's thousands of dollars!

Must've been left by Muriel's gang . . .I've heard they used to be around here.

Now you won't need to do that job.

You don't know me. It ain't robbery altogether . . .it's revenge! I'll need your help. . .then off to Texas!

What'll we do with this? Bury it again?

Yes, but not here. We'll take it to my den. . . Number Two. . . under the cross.

I nearly forgot. That pick and shovel had fresh earth on them. Who could have brought them here? Reckon they could be upstairs?

Tom and Huck had been so happy. Here at last was real treasure! But they were terrified when they heard Injun Joe coming up the stairs.

Then the rotted wood gave way. . . .

Curse the darned luck!

If there's anybody up there. . . who cares? It'll be dark in fifteen minutes. . .let 'em follow us if they want to.

I guess you're right.

Feeling safe, Tom and Huck watched Injun Joe and his friend move toward the river with the box of gold.

Whew! Wonder what he meant. . . den Number Two. . . under the cross?

They did not follow. They were happy to have reached ground without broken necks. They walked toward the town.

We'll keep a lookout for Injun Joe if he comes to town. Then we'll follow him to where they've buried the box.

He said something about revenge. What if he means us, Huck?

Oh, don't! Let's not even think about it!

Before long, though, Injun Joe and the treasure lost their importance. Becky had returned, and. . . .

I'm so glad to be back, Tom! Now, don't forget my picnic tomorrow! Papa's rented the old ferryboat!

I wouldn't miss it for anything!

Next day, as the children gathered for the picnic. . . .

You'll not get back till late. Perhaps you'd better stay all night with some of the girls who live near the ferry landing.

I'll stay with Suzy Harper, mamma.

Say. . .'stead of going to the Harper's, let's stop at the Widow Douglas's. She'll have ice cream!

The group went toward the ferryboat.

I shouldn't, but. . .it will be fun!

Three miles below town, they all went ashore. After the games and the feast. . . .

Who's ready for the cave?

Carrying candles, they
all entered the cave.
Soon they were having
fun playing hide-and-
seek in the winding
halls of the cave.

By the time they came wandering
out of the cave, they were amazed
to find that it was night.

That same night,
Huck was keeping a
lookout for Injun Joe
and his friend. Shortly
after midnight . . .

That's them!
I'll follow
them!

They went up the hill, past Welshman Jones's house, to the Widow Douglas's.

Her husband was justice of the peace. . .had me whipped! He's dead, but I'll take my revenge on her! I'll cut her nose. . .slit her ears!

Huck sped to Welshman Jones.

Somethin' terrible is going to happen to Widow Douglas! You've got to help!

Three minutes later, the old man and his sons, well-armed, were up the hill. There was an explosion of guns and a cry. Huck ran away.

Next morning, Huck again went to the Jones house.

I was awful scared when the pistols went off. I've come now because I wanted to know about it. Are them devils dead?

No, they got away. The sheriff and a group of men are going to search the woods for them.

Please don't tell it was me that told on 'em! Please!

All right if you say it Huck, but you ought to have the reward for what you did.

The same morning, at church, Aunt Polly spoke to Mrs. Harper and Mrs. Thatcher.

Did Tom stay at your house last night, Mrs. Harper?

No, he didn't.

Neither did Becky. What could have happened to them?

Tom and Becky were definitely missing. And when the children were questioned. . . .

Nobody saw them on the ferryboat going home.

Maybe they're still in the cave.

In half an hour, two hundred men were going toward the cave. For three days the search went on.

All we could find was this bit of ribbon.

It's my Becky's! She was wearing it when I saw her last! Oh. . . .

On the day of the picnic, in the cave, Tom and Becky had wandered away from the other children.

They saw many wonders.

Look!

Ugh! Bats!

Let's go down here! I've never seen this part of the cave before!

Time passed quickly, and. . . .

I wonder how long we've been down here, Tom. We better start back.

Yes, I reckon we better.

But after a while. . . .

Becky, I . . . I can't find the way. It's all mixed up.

Tom, we're lost! We'll never get out of this awful place! Why did we ever leave the others?

For hours they wandered, until they came to a place with a spring.

Becky, can you bear it if I tell you something? We must stay here where there's water to drink. This little piece of candle is our last!

Tom! Do you think they'll miss us and hunt for us?

Certainly they will! I bet they're hunting for us now. I hope they are.

They watched their bit of candle burn away, saw the tiny flame on the last inch of wick. . .and then the horror of complete darkness took over.

They slept, woke, slept again, and became hungry. The hours passed. At last Tom decided to look down some side passages. To find his way back, he unwound a kite line he found in his pocket.

He got down on his knees, feeling the way. . .then saw a human hand, holding a candle, appear from behind a rock!

Tom shouted when he saw the hand belonged to Injun Joe!

Injun Joe ran away and disappeared. Tom, scared, returned to Becky.

On Tuesday, Becky was weak with hunger. Tom went looking around.

What did you see, Tom?

N-nothing. I just shouted for luck. Let's go back.

It's our last chance.

In the third passage he tried, as he was about to give up. . . .

Looks like daylight!

We're saved! Now to get Becky.

Rushing toward the light, he pushed through a small hole. There was the Mississippi River rolling by!

After they made their way out, some men came along in a small rowboat and took them home.

A few weeks later, Tom stopped at Becky's house. Her father, Judge Thatcher, spoke to him.

Tom, nobody will get lost in that cave anymore. I had the big door covered with iron, and triple-locked.

Oh, Judge, Injun Joe's in the cave!

The news quickly spread, and before long a crowd was at the cave. When they unlocked the door, they found Injun Joe ...he had starved to death.

The morning after Injun Joe's funeral, Tom and Huck had a private talk.

Huck, that money Injun Joe found in the haunted house... it's in the cave! Will you help me get it?

You bet I will! But how will we get in?

Through that hole Becky and me came out of. I'll take you right to it in a rowboat. We'll need some kite strings, so's we can find our way back. And candles, and bags for the money, and some bread and meat.

Let's start right off, Tom!

Here...the best hole in this country... just what we need when we start our robber gang.

Who'll we rob, Tom?

Oh, most anybody. Hide them in the cave till they raise enough money for us to let them free.

Why, it's real bully, Tom. I believe it's better than to be a pirate.

Tom led the way to the place where Injun Joe had appeared.

See the cross made with candle smoke? And remember what Injun Joe said, "Under the cross." The money's got to be here!

Let's git out of here! Injun Joe's ghost is around about there, certain!

Pooh! Ghosts don't hang around where there's a cross!

Feeling safer, they searched the halls leading from the rock. They found nothing. Then....

Look! Footprints and candle grease on the clay at this side! Bet the money is under the rock! I'm going to dig in the clay!

Hey, Huck! Hear that? I've hit wood!

Tom dug about four inches, and....

We'll lift up these boards, and. . . .

There's an opening underneath!

They had uncovered a natural crack in the rock. They crawled in, followed its winding course, and. . . .

My goodness, Huck, looky here!

It's Injun Joe's den, all right!

It's the treasure box!

And some pistols, and some other stuff! We can use the pistols for our robber gang!

Got it at last! My, but we're rich, Tom!

I always knew we'd get it!

Good thing we brought these sacks . . .the box is too heavy. Let's hurry and take the money to the boat.

At sunset they reached shore and put the sacks in a wagon.

Put these old rags over 'em. We'll hide the money in the Widow's woodshed. In the morning we'll hunt up a place in the woods where it will be safe.

But when they stopped to rest near Welshman Jones's house. . . .

Come with me, boys, you're keeping everybody waiting. Hurry! What've you got there bricks or old metal?

Old metal.

Where are you taking us? And why?

To the Widow Douglas. You'll see why when we get there.

At the Widow's, everybody of any importance in town was there.

Tom wasn't at home, but I found him and Huck right at my door.

Come with me, boys.

The two boys were rushed upstairs, where they changed into new clothes the Widow had bought them. Then everyone sat down to supper, with the children at little side tables.

The Widow had learned of Huck's part in saving her from Injun Joe, and now she had something to say.

I'm going to give Huckleberry a home with me, and get him educated. And some day I'll start him in a small business.

Huck don't need it. . . he's rich! Oh you needn't smile. . .just wait a minute!

Tom rushed out, returned with the sacks, and told how he and Huck had found the treasure.

See? What did I tell you? Half is Huck's and half is mine!

And when the money was counted. . . .

It amounts to a little over $12,000. Tom's right. . .he and Huck are rich!

60

The boys' good luck caused a lot of excitement. Wherever they went, they were stared at and admired.

There they go. . . the boys who found the treasure!

Huck lived with the Widow, who taught him polite ways.

Use your fork, Huck.

I can't stand livin' like this. She means well, but. . . .

After three weeks, he ran off. Tom found him in an old empty barrel behind an empty building.

Better go back, Huck. . .the Widow's awful worried.

She's good to me, Tom . . .but I can't stand them ways!

I got to wash, and comb, and wear them darn clothes. She won't let me smoke, or chew tobacco, or yell, or scratch. . .and she prays all the time! It ain't for me. . .I ain't used to it!

Darn it! Just as we was all fixed to turn robbers with a cave and all, this trouble had to come up!

Oh, being rich ain't going to keep me from turning robber!

You mean it, Tom?

Sure! But I can't let you into the gang if you ain't got a home. A robber is more high-toned than a pirate.

We'll start the gang tonight! We'll meet at midnight, and swear on a coffin to stand by each other, and sign it with blood!

That's something I like! Tom, I'll stick to the Widow till I rot. And if I get to be a great robber, and everybody talks about it, I reckon she'll be proud!

Well, I'll go back to the Widow for a month and see if I can stand it, if you'll let me in the gang.

All right, Huck! Come along, and I'll ask the Widow to let up on you a bit.

THE END